Nick Ford Mysteries

The Night of the Loch Ness Monster

by
Jerry Stemach

Don Johnston Incorporated
Volo, Illinois

Edited by:

Jerry Stemach, MS, CCC-SLP
AAC Specialist, Adaptive Technology Center, Sonoma County, California

Gail Portnuff Venable, MS, CCC-SLP
Speech-Language Pathologist, Scottish Rite Center for Childhood Language Disorders, San Francisco, California

Dorothy Tyack, MA
Learning Disabilities Specialist, Scottish Rite Center for Childhood Language Disorders, San Francisco, California

Consultant:

Ted S. Hasselbring, PhD
Professor of Special Education, Vanderbilt University, Nashville, TN

Cover Design and Illustration: Jeff Hamm, Karyl Shields

Interior Illustrations: Jeff Hamm

Published by:

Don Johnston Incorporated
26799 West Commerce Drive
Volo, IL 60073

DON JOHNSTON

Printed in the U.S.A. No part of this publication may be reproduced, stored in a retrieval system or transmitted in any form or by any means electronic, mechanical photocopying recording, or otherwise.

International Standard Book Number
ISBN 1-893376-40-0

Contents

A Note from the Start-to-Finish Editors

**This book is for my dad,
Joe Stemach.
He reads something new,
every day.**

Many people have contributed to
The Night of the Loch Ness Monster.
My wife, Beverly, my daughter, Kristie,
and my father, Joseph Stemach, who
went to Scotland with me.
My friends and colleagues
Gail Portnuff Venable and Dorothy Tyack
Alan Venable
Rachel Whitaker
The entire staff at Don Johnston Incorporated
TK Audio
Kevin Feldman
Michael Benedetti, Michael Sturgeon
Melia Dicker, Sarah Stemach
Robert Berta, photographer
and the good people of the Highlands in Scotland.

Chapter 1

The Wrong Way

Ken Rice unlocked the door of a new green van. "Hey!" yelled Ken. "Someone stole our steering wheel!"

Jeff and Kris Ford laughed. Their dad, Nick Ford, laughed, too. Jeff put his hands over his mouth and said, "This is Planet Earth calling Ken Rice. Planet Earth calling Ken Rice."

"Think about this, Ken," said Kris. "We just landed in Glasgow, Scotland. People here drive on the other side of the road."

"You mean the wrong side of the road," Ken said. "At least they could leave the steering wheel alone."

"Does this mean that you don't want to drive first?" asked Nick.

"I'm not driving first, last, or in the middle," said Ken.

"Toss me the keys," Kris told Ken. "You sit up front next to me and read the map. We need to get to Loch Ness before dark," she said.

"Where's Mandy?" asked Nick.

"I'll go and find her," said Jeff.

Mandy Ming, Ken Rice, and Jeff and Kris Ford were best friends. They all went to City College of New York. Nick Ford was a biology teacher at the college. Nick and the kids were in Scotland because Nick was helping to set up the new Loch Ness Monster Visitors' Center. Nick had asked the kids to help him set up a display about dinosaurs at the Center.

"Wait," said Kris. "Here comes Mandy."

Mandy was holding a plastic bag.

"Are you shopping already?" Jeff asked her. "We just got off the plane!"

Mandy smiled at Jeff. "Just for that, you can't have any of the shortbread cookies that I bought," she said. "And for your information, I bought a book about the Loch Ness monster and a really good book of maps for backpacking in the Highlands." Mandy put the book of maps into Jeff's backpack.

"Well," said Jeff. "Maybe I don't want a cookie that is short and maybe I don't want a cookie that tastes like bread."

Nick laughed. "You will eat those words, Jeff. Shortbread cookies are fantastic."

Everyone got into the van. Ken sat in the front next to Kris. "I'm sitting in the driver's seat, but there's no steering wheel," he said. "This is too weird."

Kris drove onto the main highway. Soon the road became narrow and steep, but people in other cars were still driving fast. "People here are good drivers," said Nick. "You won't see people here going through red lights like they do in New York."

"That's because there aren't any red lights here to go through," said Ken. "Just steep mountains."

"I can see why they call this part of Scotland 'the Highlands,' " said Mandy. "There are high hills and mountains everywhere."

"Yes," said Nick. "And there are sheep on nearly every mountain. There are more sheep in Scotland than there are people."

Mandy got out the shortbread cookies. Then she turned to Nick and asked, "So what do you think, Nick? Is there really a Loch Ness monster?"

Chapter 2

The Monster Attacks

DIPLODOCUS

"I'll tell you about the Loch Ness monster," said Nick. "But it will cost you a shortbread cookie."

"OK," said Mandy. "But no cookie for Jeff. He's mean." Jeff was Mandy's boyfriend, and she liked to tease him.

Nick spoke. "First, let me tell you that a scientist needs proof before saying that something is real. I know that this cookie that I'm eating is real because I can touch it and study it."

Jeff laughed. "If I promise to be good, Mandy, will you let me touch and study one of your cookies?" he asked.

Before Mandy could answer Jeff's question, Ken said, "Give Jeff a cookie. Then maybe the man will shut up long enough for Nick to tell us about the monster."

Nick spoke again. "No one has ever touched the Loch Ness monster," he said. "But over 1,000 people have said that they've seen it. Some people have even taken pictures of Nessie. You'll hear the stories and see the pictures at the Visitors' Center."

"Who's Nessie?" asked Kris.

"Nessie is the monster's nickname," said Jeff.

Mandy spoke to Nick again. "You still haven't told us what *you* think, Nick. Do *you* believe in the monster?"

"Well, I believe in dinosaurs," said Nick. "We have bones from dinosaurs. When we put some of the dinosaur bones together to make a dinosaur skeleton, the skeleton looks a lot like the pictures of the Loch Ness monster."

"Are you saying that Nessie is a dinosaur?" asked Mandy.

"If Nessie is real, it could be a dinosaur that got trapped in Loch Ness," Nick answered.

"What does this thing look like?" asked Jeff.

Mandy reached into her bag and took out her book on the Loch Ness monster. "Let me show you the most famous photograph of the Loch Ness monster," she said. "This picture was taken in 1954."

Nick looked at the picture. "That looks like a dinosaur called 'Diplodocus,'" he said.

"It was the biggest of all the dinosaurs that ate plants. 'Diplodocus' had legs, not flippers, but they may be related."

Kris drove through a city called Fort William. Ken looked at the map. "It won't be much farther now," he said.

Kris drove another 30 minutes before they finally came to Loch Ness.

"That is one huge lake," said Jeff.

"Yes," said Nick. "Loch Ness is 24 miles long, up to one mile wide, and 1,000 feet deep. It's the biggest lake in all of Scotland and England."

The road went closer to the lake. As Kris turned a corner, she suddenly slammed on the brakes. An old woman was standing in the middle of the road waving her hands. The woman looked as if she had seen a ghost. She was crying.

Ken rolled down his window.

"Won't you please help me?" the lady asked. "It's my husband! My poor husband," she cried. "I think that he's dead."

"What happened?" asked Ken.

"It's the monster!" she said.

"We saw the monster!"

Chapter 3

Heart Attack

Everyone got out of the car and followed the old woman down a trail to a rocky beach next to the lake. A man was lying near the water. Mandy could see that the man and woman had stopped here for a picnic. There was a picnic basket and a blanket on the ground. The man's legs were on the blanket but his head was in a patch of mud and rocks. He didn't move.

"He may have had a heart attack," said Nick.

Kris and Mandy knelt down next to the man. Kris shook him and shouted, "Are you OK?" The man didn't move. Next, Kris put her head close to the man's face. Then she looked up at Nick. "I don't think he's breathing," she said.

Nick gently pulled the man back onto the blanket and turned him onto his back. "OK, girls," said Nick. "This is just like your CPR class. Only this time, it's for real."

Mandy and Kris knew exactly what to do.

Mandy knelt down and tilted the man's head back. Then she gently pinched his nose shut and put her lips tightly around his mouth. She blew two slow breaths into his mouth. Nick watched the air go into the man's chest. Then Mandy checked to see if the man's heart was beating. "No pulse!" said Mandy.

Kris was also kneeling next to the man. She placed her hands on his chest in just the right way.

Mandy said, "Begin CPR!"

Kris began to push down against the man's chest five times with her hands. She counted out loud each time that she pushed. "One and…two and…three and…four and…five!" When Kris got to five, Mandy gave the man another slow breath of air with her mouth.

Ken, Jeff, and Nick watched the girls. Ken put his arm around the old woman.

After just one minute of CPR, the man began to cough. Mandy could hear him suck in air and start to breathe on his own. The man tried to speak, but Kris told him not to talk.

The old woman called out to her husband. "Angus, Angus, these girls have saved your life!"

Nick spoke quickly to the woman. "My name is Nick Ford, but I don't think that I heard your name."

"Mary," said the woman. "My name is Mary Maclean."

"We haven't saved Angus yet," said
Nick. "We need to get him to the
emergency room at the hospital as fast
as we can."

Nick spoke to Jeff and Ken. "I want
you boys to help Angus up to the van,"
said Nick. "The girls and I will take
Mary and Angus to the hospital in
Fort William."

"Do you want us to go with you?"
asked Jeff.

Nick thought for a moment. Then
he answered. "No. Something bad
happened here tonight.

I want to know what Angus and Mary saw out there. Get Angus into the van, and then grab your backpacks. I think you two boys better spend the night right here."

Chapter 4

The Night of the
Loch Ness Monster

Ken and Jeff took their backpacks down to the shore of Loch Ness. It was dark, but there was a bright moon in the sky. Ken glanced far down the shoreline while Jeff looked at the water right in front of him.

"Do you see what I see?" asked Ken.

"Yes," said Jeff. "I wonder how it got there."

Ken thought for a moment. "I'll bet that it's been there for 500 years!" he said.

Jeff laughed quietly. "Are you looking at the same thing that I'm looking at?" Jeff asked. "I'm looking at that little patch of oil on the water. What are you looking at?"

Ken laughed, too. "I'm looking at that castle down there." Ken pointed at a cliff that was about half a mile away.

"Now that's way cool," said Jeff. As the boys looked at the castle, they saw a tiny red light. The light seemed to come from the top of an old tower that was part of the castle.

"It's a signal light!" yelled Ken.

"Not so fast," said Jeff. "It's probably just a bunch of kids fooling around."

"Well, you can stay here and watch some oily water," said Ken. "I'm going to hike down there to the castle and check out that light."

Jeff grabbed Ken's arm. "Do you remember Nick's rule?" asked Jeff.

"Nick has a million rules," answered Ken. "Which one?"

"You know which one," said Jeff. "The one that says, 'Be safe. Don't go off by yourself.' Besides, Nick wants us to stay here and see if Nessie shows up again."

Ken opened his backpack and took out two walkie-talkies. He handed one to Jeff. "I'm not exactly going off by myself," said Ken. "If something comes up, page me."

"Oh, sure!" said Jeff. "If something comes up, page you! If something comes up, it will be a 50-foot monster that can give a guy a heart attack!"

Ken laughed at Jeff. "If that monster gets you, I'll whup him the way that Muhammad Ali whupped Joe Frazier," he said.

Jeff watched as Ken walked away. Jeff looked at the castle. He could still see the red light turning on and off. "That light is going on and off every ten seconds," Jeff said to himself. "Maybe Ken is right. Maybe it is a signal!"

Jeff looked back at the water by his feet. In the moonlight he could see that the oil was still floating there.

Jeff took a plastic jar out of his

backpack and took a sample of the oily

water. "Maybe there is a clue here,"

he thought.

Jeff put the top on the jar and then

wrote on the label.

WATER SAMPLE FROM

LOCH NESS SHORE BY

ANGUS AND MARY'S PICNIC SPOT

JUNE 12

11:20 p.m.

Jeff put the jar into his backpack.

Then he looked toward the castle.

Suddenly, Jeff froze. He blinked his

eyes. There! Just off the shore from

the castle! It was the Loch Ness

monster! Jeff could see its head

sticking up ten feet out of the water!

Chapter 5

Inside the Castle

Jeff watched as the Loch Ness monster sank back into the water and disappeared. He took the walkie-talkie off of his belt and spoke into it. "Ken! Ken! Are you there?" he shouted. There was no answer. Jeff tried again. "Talk to me, Ken," he said. But there was still no answer.

Jeff couldn't see the red signal light at the castle anymore. He opened his pack and grabbed a flashlight. Next to the flashlight, he saw Mandy's book of maps.

"There's the book that Mandy bought at the airport," he said to himself. "Boy, am I glad that she likes to shop!"

Jeff opened the book and found Loch Ness. It was easy to find the old castle that Ken wanted to explore. "Urquhart Castle," Jeff said to himself. "Urquhart Castle, here I come." On the next page, there was a map that showed all of the buildings and artifacts at the castle. The castle was now a park for visitors.

Jeff hiked along the shore of the lake. He could see that part of the castle went right down to the water. There was a deep, wide ditch that went around the castle. Jeff looked at the ditch and thought, "That's the old moat. A long time ago, they kept water in the moat so that no one could attack the castle." Jeff saw that there was a wooden bridge across the moat. He knew that if he wanted to go into the castle, he would have to cross that bridge.

"If there are people in the castle, they will see me crossing the bridge," Jeff said. "But I don't see any other way to get inside."

Jeff put on his black sweatshirt. Next he rubbed mud on his hands and face so that it would be hard to see him. When he was ready, Jeff moved slowly toward the bridge.

Urquhart Castle looked cold and lonely in the moonlight. Jeff stood still and watched the castle, but he didn't see anyone.

Just as he started to move again, he spotted Ken's walkie-talkie. It was lying in the middle of the bridge! "No wonder he didn't answer me," thought Jeff.

Jeff grabbed the walkie-talkie and ran across the bridge. Just as he got inside the castle, he heard a loud grinding noise behind him. He turned around and looked back. A huge gate was coming down! The gate was made out of heavy steel spikes! Jeff would be trapped inside! He raced back toward the gate.

Now Jeff was ten feet away and the gate was only two feet from touching the ground. Jeff dove onto the ground and slid under the gate. He dropped his flashlight and watched it fall off the bridge and into the moat. He felt one of the spikes hit his shoe. Jeff pulled on his foot with all his might. He pulled his foot right out of his shoe. Then he stood up and ran away from the castle as fast as he could!

Chapter 6

An Emergency Call

Jeff ran up a hill to the visitors' parking lot. He found a pay phone in a small building next to the parking lot. Jeff picked up the phone and dialed '0' for the operator but no one answered. Next he dialed '9-1-1.' Still nothing happened. "Maybe you have to put money in first," he said. Jeff took some coins from his pocket. Some of the coins were dimes and quarters from the U.S., and some of them were five-pence and ten-pence coins from Britain. It was dark inside the phone booth and Jeff could not tell the coins apart.

Finally, Jeff just started putting all of the coins into the phone. He dialed '9-1-1' again, but no one answered. Now Jeff was angry. He started hitting the '9' over and over. Suddenly, a man's voice answered.

"This is the 9-9-9 emergency operator. Can I help you?" asked the man.

"Yes!" shouted Jeff. "I need to talk with Mr. Nick Ford at the hospital in Fort William right away."

"I can connect you," said the man.

In less than a minute, Jeff heard Nick's voice.

"Dad! It's me!" said Jeff.

"Where are you, son?" asked Nick.

"I'm in the parking lot at the Urquhart Castle," Jeff answered. "I saw the monster and now I think Ken has been kidnapped!"

"I already know about Ken," said Nick. "You sit tight and we'll pick you up in 30 minutes."

"I have to get the backpacks," said Jeff. "Meet me back at the place where we found Mary and Angus." Then Jeff hung up the phone.

When Nick drove up in the van, he had Kris and Mandy with him. Two other men were also in the van.

Mandy jumped out and gave Jeff a hug. "What happened to you?" she asked. "You're filthy."

"Never mind about me," said Jeff. "What about Ken?"

"Nick will tell you," said Mandy. "Hop in."

When Jeff got into the van, Nick introduced the other men. "Jeff, I want you to meet George MacDonald. George is the one who invited us here. He's the director of the Loch Ness Monster Visitors' Center.

George shook Jeff's hand and said, "I'm terribly sorry about Ken. I'm afraid that I'm responsible for this bit of bad luck."

The other man shook Jeff's hand, also. "I'm Constable Gordon," he said. "I'm the chief of police in Fort William."

Jeff nodded at the men. "So where's Ken?" he asked.

Constable Gordon spoke. "It's not good news, I'm afraid," he said. "Ken has been kidnapped all right. He called us on a cell phone. He wasn't allowed to say much, but he seemed to be OK. The people who are holding him said that they would call us back in 24 hours. We don't know what they want yet."

6 of 7

"What about Angus Maclean?" asked Jeff.

"The doctor said that Angus will pull through," said Kris. "He needs to rest."

Nick spoke. "We asked Angus and Mary not to say anything about seeing a monster. If a reporter hears about it, the story will be in every newspaper in the world by tomorrow morning."

Chapter 7

The Secret Message

While Nick drove the van back toward Fort William, Jeff told everyone about the monster and the red signal light.   He told them about Ken's walkie-talkie on the bridge.   And he told them about the gate at the castle.

Constable Gordon listened carefully. "Think hard," he said to Jeff.   "Was there anything else?"

Jeff thought.   Then he remembered the oil on the water.   He reached into his pack and got out the sample of water.

"Where could we have that water
tested?" Nick asked the constable.

"We send all of our crime samples
to a lab over in the capital," said
Constable Gordon.

"Isn't Edinburgh the capital of
Scotland?" asked Mandy.

"Right you are," said the constable.
"It's about a three-hour drive from
here."

The constable took a piece of paper
out of his pocket and handed it to Jeff.
"Take a look at this, Jeff," he said.

"These are the exact words that Ken said to us on the phone. We think that it's a secret code because he didn't use his real name. He said that his name was David Livingstone."

"David Livingstone?" asked Jeff. "Wasn't David Livingstone a famous explorer?"

"Yes," said George. "He was born in Scotland. While your country was busy fighting the Civil War, David Livingstone was exploring the Nile River in Africa."

Jeff took the paper and read the words on it.

"Hi Nick. I'm OK.

This is David Livingstone.

It's about 10 after 2.

Give Eddie B. a message.

Treasure Island is on TV

at 5 o'clock on Friday.

"What does it mean?" asked Jeff.

"We were hoping that you could tell us," said Mandy.

"Ken was wrong about the time, too," said Kris. "He called us at 12:30."

Jeff thought. "What's that stuff about Treasure Island?"

"Well, it's not on TV this Friday," said Mandy. "We checked the newspaper."

"Great Scott!" George replied, "Treasure Island was written by Robert Louis Stevenson. He was born and raised in Edinburgh."

"That's what 'Eddie B' stands for!" Kris shouted. "Eddie B stands for Edinburgh!"

Jeff smiled. "Ken has been watching too many spy movies," he said. "But it sounds as if something important is happening on Friday. That's the day after tomorrow."

"The meeting place has something to do with Treasure Island," said Kris. "But I still don't get the part about David Livingstone."

Nick drove the van to the police station. Everyone went inside.

"Let's talk about what we should do tomorrow," said Nick. "Our number one job is to get Ken back. Jeff, you and the constable go and explore every inch of Urquhart Castle. If Ken is still there, you must find him! I'll go with George in his boat," said Nick. "We will check out the water by the castle. George and I think the monster that Jeff saw is a big fake," Nick said.

"Someone is going to a lot of trouble to get some attention," said George.

"They gave Angus Maclean a heart attack," said Kris.

"If it's the same people who kidnapped Ken, then they have broken the law," said the constable.

"What do you want Kris and me to do?" asked Mandy.

"I want you girls to drive to Edinburgh," said Nick. "Take the water sample to the lab there. Find out why Ken was talking about Treasure Island."

Chapter 8

Under the Boat

The next morning, Constable Gordon gave everyone cell phones so that they could call each other at any time. Then Jeff and Constable Gordon went to Urquhart Castle. Kris and Mandy dropped Nick off at the Visitors' Center and then they drove to Edinburgh.

Nick met his friend George at the boat dock. Nick laughed when he saw the name that was painted on the back of George's boat. The boat was named 'Curious George.'

"That's the name of a monkey in a children's book," thought Nick. "The monkey was always getting into trouble because he liked to explore things."

"Good morning, George," yelled Nick as he jumped into the big white boat.

George waved to Nick and backed the boat away from the dock.

Nick looked around. "This boat is crammed with scientific equipment," he said.

"I used this boat during 'Operation Deepscan,' " said George.

"What was Operation Deepscan?" asked Nick.

"In 1987, we had 24 boats on Loch Ness that were just like mine," answered George. He pointed up at a big piece of equipment that was on top of the roof. "Each boat had sonar equipment on it," he said.

"What does sonar do?" asked Nick.

"It can show you a picture of what is under the water," said George.

"The sonar equipment sends sounds through the water. If the sound hits something under the water, it will bounce back to my boat and show me a picture."

George pointed to a small green TV screen next to the steering wheel.

"In Operation Deepscan, we lined up the 24 boats next to each other. Then we went slowly up and down Loch Ness, watching our TV screens. We each watched our TV screens to see if we could find the Loch Ness monster."

"Did you find it?" asked Nick.

"We think so," said George. "We found something very big that was swimming about 200 feet under water."

George slowed down the boat and turned on the sonar equipment and his TV screen. Nick could see small shapes moving across the screen. "What are those?" asked Nick.

"Fish," said George. "There are enough fish in Loch Ness to feed a big monster like Nessie."

Nick could see Urquhart Castle by the shoreline.

"This is the place where Saint Columba saw the Loch Ness monster in the year 565," George told Nick. "Saint Columba said that the monster was attacking one of his men."

"Well," said Nick. "Saints are supposed to tell the truth!"

George laughed. "Yes, and priests are supposed to tell the truth, also. In 1971, a priest named Father Gregory saw the monster near here. Lots of people believe Father Gregory."

"Do you believe him?" asked Nick.

"Yes, I do," George answered. "There's a monster in this lake. I'm sure of it. I just hope that I live long enough to see it."

Nick looked down at the TV screen. Something very, very large was moving across the screen.

"Look!" yelled Nick. "What is that?"

George looked at the screen. "Great Scott!" he yelled. "I don't know what it is, but it's right under the boat!"

Chapter 9

Nick Meets the Monster

George yelled at Nick. "Get your camera! Whatever that thing is, it's coming to the top!"

Nick was excited as he reached for his camera bag. Suddenly, there was a loud bang! The boat shook. Something was pushing against the bottom of the boat. Nick lost his grip on the bag. He watched it fly through the air and fall into the lake with a splash.

George yelled. "No, Nick! Stop!" But it was too late. Nick was already diving into the lake!

George watched the TV screen. The big shape was moving away, but there was still a smaller shape under the boat. It was Nick. George watched as Nick came up out of the water at the back of the boat. "Let's chase it, George!" yelled Nick, as he climbed into the boat.

George pushed on the throttle for more speed. The boat leaped ahead in the water. Nick nearly fell back into the lake.

"I see it!" called George.   "But it's going deeper."   Nick staggered up to George and looked at the TV screen. He could see the shape getting smaller and smaller as it went deeper and deeper into the lake.

George tapped the TV screen.   "The monster is 750 feet deep now and still going down."   Nick looked at the TV screen, but the shape was gone.

"We lost him!" yelled George.

"We didn't lose all of him," said Nick.

"What do you mean?" asked George.

Nick held up an eyeball that was the size of a tennis ball. "Great Scott!" yelled George.

"At last we have something that we can touch and study," said Nick. "This is what I call real science."

Nick handed the eyeball to George. "There's just one little problem," said Nick. "This eyeball is made out of glass."

"The monster is a fake!" said George.

"Yes," said Nick. "But the person inside of the monster is not fake. And the people who have kidnapped Ken are not fakes." Nick pointed to the castle. "Take us over there, George."

George steered the boat close to the castle, and then turned off the motor.

"I wonder if Ken is in there," said Nick.

"If the stones in that castle were alive, the stones could tell us," said George. "The stones could tell us what happened to Ken."

Nick nodded his head. "Yes, if that castle were made out of living stones, then..." Nick did not finish his sentence. "Living stones, living stones," Nick said again.

George looked at Nick. "Great Scott!" shouted George. "Living stones!" That's what Ken meant when he said that he was David Livingstone!

He was trying to tell us about a certain stone in the castle!"

"But what did Ken say next?" asked Nick.

George tried hard to remember. "I think that Ken said it was about 10 after 2," George answered.

"I don't think Ken was talking about the time," said Nick. "I think that he was trying to tell us that there was a clue on one of the stones. 10 numbers after the number 2 is 12!"

Chapter 10

Mr. Tevvy

George started up his boat and handed a cell phone to Nick. "Call Jeff and Constable Gordon," said George. "Tell them about the clue. Tell them to look for something with a number 12. I want to get you some dry clothes at the Visitors' Center because I'm afraid you'll freeze to death."

"The water in that lake is pretty cold," said Nick.

Nick called Jeff and told him about the eyeball and about Ken's clue.

"Sometimes you do some pretty stupid things, Dad," said Jeff.

Nick laughed. "Just don't tell your old Dad to 'Go jump in the lake,' " said Nick. "George and I will be at the Loch Ness Monster Visitors' Center."

As George drove the boat up to the dock, Nick looked at the Visitors' Center. Many people were working on the new building.

"This place is huge!" said Nick.

"Yes," said George. "One of the biggest rooms will have your dinosaur display in it."

"How much did all of this cost?" Nick asked George.

"It will cost about a million pounds by the time it's finished," said George.

"Help me out here," said Nick. "I know that in Scotland your money is called pounds and in the U.S. our money is called dollars. I know that one pound is worth more than one dollar."

"It will cost close to two million dollars," said George.

Nick thought for a minute before he spoke. "Can I ask you where you got all that money?" said Nick.

"Most of the money is coming from a man that I have never met," answered George. "His name is Richard Tevvy. He will own 90% of the Loch Ness Visitors' Center."

"I guess we could call him 'Rich' for short," said Nick.

George laughed. "Mr. Tevvy is rich all right. In 1994 he discovered oil off the west coast of Scotland.

Now Mr. Tevvy is a rich man and Scotland is becoming a rich nation from his oil. Mr. Tevvy uses his money to buy TV stations, newspapers, and things like the Visitors' Center here."

Nick thought about what George said. "What would be the best thing that could happen at Loch Ness to get more people to come to the Visitors' Center?" asked Nick.

"Seeing the Loch Ness monster!" said George. "That would make a lot of people come here."

"And who would get the most money if all those people came here?" asked Nick.

"Mr. Tevvy would get the most money because he owns most of the center," said George.

"Think about it, George," said Nick. "Mr. Tevvy owns his own newspapers and TV stations. If someone said that they saw the Loch Ness monster, Mr. Tevvy could be the first one to put the story in a newspaper. Other newspapers would buy the story from him.

People would read the story, come here, and pay to get into the Visitors' Center!"

"Great Scott!" yelled George. "I'll bet that Mr. Tevvy brought the fake monster to Loch Ness!"

Chapter 11

Treasure Island

"I think that the fake monster is Mr. Tevvy's idea," said Nick. "Do you remember what Ken said to us?

'Give Eddie B. a message. Treasure Island is on TV at 5 o'clock on Friday.'

I think that 'TV' is short for Tevvy," said Nick. "I think that Ken's message really means this:

Go to Edinburgh.

There will be a meeting at

Treasure Island.

The meeting at Treasure Island is on.

Mr. Tevvy will meet someone there at

5 o'clock on Friday."

Just then, Nick's cell phone rang.

It was Mandy. "The lab just finished

the test on the oil," she said. "The lab

said that it's a very special oil. It is not

the kind that is used in small boats.

It's called 'high-grade' oil. It is used

mostly in scientific equipment.

The people at the lab asked us if anyone was using an underwater camera or a submarine to explore Loch Ness."

"The people at the lab made a good guess," said Nick. "The monster that Jeff saw is a fake. It must be part of a tiny submarine. George says that there are submarines that hold one or two people."

"Wow," said Mandy. "Now what do we do?"

"Did you find out anything about Treasure Island?" asked Nick.

"Yes," said Mandy. "When Robert Louis Stevenson was a little boy, his family lived in a house across the street from the Queen Street Gardens in Edinburgh. The gardens are like a big park. There is a small lake in the gardens. Robert could see the lake from his bedroom window. In the middle of the lake is a little island. People call it 'Treasure Island' because it gave Robert the idea for his book about pirates. Isn't that a cute story?" she asked.

"Yes," said Nick. "And I think that there will be a meeting of real pirates tomorrow afternoon at 5 o'clock. I want you and Kris to stay in Edinburgh tonight. Meet us in the Queen Street Gardens tomorrow at 4:30. Bring a reporter from the London Times newspaper with you. But don't let anyone see you there. There's a chance that Ken will be back with us by then."

As soon as Nick ended the call, his phone rang again. This time it was Jeff.

Jeff sounded angry. "Your phone doesn't work, and George's phone has been busy," said Jeff.

"My phone got wet, remember?" said Nick. "What's up?" he asked.

"You and George need to get over here to Urquhart Castle as fast as you can," said Jeff. "We found number 12."

Chapter 12

The Secret Cave

Jeff met Nick and George in the parking lot at the castle. Constable Gordon was talking to the people at the ticket booth. "No more visitors today," said the constable. "We're working on a crime here."

Jeff and Constable Gordon led everyone down the hill. They walked across the bridge that went over the moat. Jeff led everyone to the tower.

"From here on, let's be quiet," Jeff said. "Just follow me. I will be stopping at the 12th step."

The men followed Jeff down the steep and narrow steps. Jeff counted the steps. "...9, 10, 11, 12," he said to himself.

Jeff stopped and reached up over his head. He put his hand between two of the stones in the wall. Nick and George heard a 'CLICK!' Then Jeff put his hands against a large stone on the wall. He pushed against the stone. It moved and swung open like a door! Jeff was standing in front of a dark, wet tunnel!

Jeff bent down and went into the tunnel. On each side of the tunnel were little rooms that were carved out of the rock. Jeff could see rusty, old chains on the floor of some of the rooms. "This was an old prison!" Jeff thought to himself.

At the end of the tunnel was a large cave where the men could stand up. George lit a match. Part of the cave was rock and part of the cave was water. No one seemed to be in the cave. Nick called Ken's name. "Ken! Are you in here? This is Nick!"

A voice groaned.

"Great Scott!" said George.   "It's Ken!   He's over here!"

George lit another match.   Ken was sitting against the wall of the cave. There was a chain on his leg and a piece of tape over his mouth.   Jeff ran to Ken and yanked off the tape.

"Ouch!" yelled Ken.   "I won't have to shave my lip for a week," he said.

"Are you OK?" asked Constable Gordon.

"I'm wet and tired and hungry.   Get me out of here," said Ken.

"Who put you in here?" asked Jeff.

"You'll see for yourselves," said Ken. "I can hear them coming."

Everyone stood still and listened. They could hear the sound of a motor.

Ken spoke again.   "Quick," he said. "There are flashlights in a box by the water.   Take all of the flashlights and hide behind the rocks!"

The men did as Ken said. The sound of the motor was louder now, but it was too dark to see anything. Soon the motor stopped. Two voices were talking. "The flashlights aren't in the box," said one voice.

Nick stood up. "That's because we have them," he said. Jeff, George, and the constable stood up, also. They all turned on the flashlights at the same time, and they couldn't believe their eyes.

There in the water was a small brown submarine that was just big enough for two people. On the sub was the long head of a monster, looking down at them. And one of the monster's eyes was missing!

Chapter 13

Under Arrest

The two men put their hands in the air. "You are both under arrest," said Constable Gordon. He pointed at Ken and said, "Unlock the chain on that man!"

One of the men went over to Ken and took off the lock.

"Who do you work for?" Nick asked the two men.

The men would not talk. "Let me try," said George. He walked up to the two men. "I know who you're working for. You're working for Richard Tevvy.

You're meeting him tomorrow at 5 o'clock in the Queen Street Gardens in Edinburgh. Am I right? You can either answer me or rot in jail," said George.

"Yes," said one of the men. "You're right. Mr. Tevvy owns this submarine. But he won't pay us now because no one will say that they saw the Loch Ness monster."

"I don't know about that," said Ken. "Mary and Angus Maclean will say that they saw the monster."

"That's a great idea," said Nick. "They can use Mr. Tevvy's money to pay for their doctor bills."

Constable Gordon spoke to George. "How would you like to have that submarine and fake monster in the new Visitors' Center?" he asked.

Jeff and Nick knew what George would say, so Jeff and Nick said it at the same time as George.   "Great Scott!"

Constable Gordon took the two men to the police station in Fort William.

The two men agreed to help catch Mr. Tevvy.

The next day, everyone met with Mary and Angus and made a plan. Then they drove to Edinburgh.

At 4:30, Nick and Jeff found Kris and Mandy near 'Treasure Island.' The girls introduced Nick and Jeff to a reporter from the London Times newspaper and a reporter from the BBC television station.

"I hope that it's OK that I got two reporters," said Kris.

Nick smiled. "It's fine with me," he said. "It will be fun to see this on TV."

The reporters put hidden microphones on the two men from the sub and on Mary and Angus. Everyone else stood behind trees and bushes and waited.

At 5 o'clock, a well-dressed man came up to the men from the sub.

"Hello, Mr. Tevvy," said one of the men. "I want you to meet Mary and Angus Maclean. They saw the Loch Ness monster and they want to tell your newspaper all about it."

"You were very lucky to see the monster," said Mr. Tevvy. "Your story will be worth a lot of money."

"Why don't you pay Mary and Angus right now?" asked one of the men.

"Well, I don't have any money to give them right now," said Mr. Tevvy.

"You can give them the 10,000 pounds that you owe us for working on the sub," said the man.

Mr. Tevvy looked around. At that moment, everyone stepped out from behind the trees and bushes. Mr. Tevvy saw the TV camera and tried to hide his face.

Nick walked up and stood next to Mr. Tevvy and patted him on the back. "I would like you all to meet the real Loch Ness monster," said Nick. "The real Loch Ness monster is Mr. Tevvy!"

Everyone started to clap.

The End

A Note from the Start-to-Finish Editors

You will notice that Start-to-Finish Books look different from
other high-low readers and chapter books. The text layout of
this book coordinates with the other media components (CD
and audiocassette) of the Start-to-Finish series.

The text in the book matches, line-for-line and page-for-page,
the text shown on the computer screen, enabling readers to
follow along easily in the book. Each page ends in a complete
sentence so that the student can either practice the page
(repeat reading) or turn the page to continue with the story.
If the next sentence cannot fit on the page in its entirety, it
has been shifted to the next page. For this reason, the
sentence at the top of a page may not be indented, signaling
that it is part of the paragraph from the preceding page.

Words are not hyphenated at the ends of lines. This
sometimes creates extra space at the end of a line, but
eliminates confusion for the struggling reader.